Black
Gold

Black Gold

Sara Cassidy

Illustrated by Helen Flook

ORCA BOOK PUBLISHERS

Library and Archives Canada Cataloguing in Publication

Cassidy, Sara, author
Black gold / Sara Cassidy ; illustrated by Helen Flook.
(Orca echoes)

Issued in print and electronic formats.
ISBN 978-1-4598-1422-6 (softcover).—ISBN 978-1-4598-1423-3 (pdf).—
ISBN 978-1-4598-1424-0 (epub)

I. Flook, Helen, illustrator II. Title. III. Series: Orca echoes
PS8555.A7812B525 2017   jc813'.54   C2017-900864-1
C2017-900865-X

First published in the United States, 2017
Library of Congress Control Number: 2017933016

Summary: In this early chapter book, the follow-up to *Blackberry Juice* and *Not For Sale*,
Cyrus and Rudy discover gold on the farm. Black gold, that is.

Orca Book Publishers gratefully acknowledges the support for its publishing programs
provided by the following agencies: the Government of Canada through the Canada Book Fund
and the Canada Council for the Arts, and the Province of British Columbia
through the BC Arts Council and the Book Publishing Tax Credit.

Edited by Liz Kemp
Cover artwork and interior illustrations by Helen Flook
Author photo by Amaya Tarasoff

ORCA BOOK PUBLISHERS
www.orcabook.com

Printed and bound in Canada.

20 19 18 17 • 4 3 2 1

In memory of Constanze,
who could hear the mosses sing.

Chapter One

Last week Rudy and I dragged an old table down to the road that wriggles like a worm past our new house.

Blackberries grow like crazy around here. I worry I'm tricking people by making them pay for something they can just reach out for. It's like selling dandelions. Or flies.

We sell the blackberries in a box that we make with a paper plate, some ninja-like folding moves and a few staples. The tomatoes we sell in brown lunch bags. Rudy folds the tops down carefully. The dahlia bouquets stand in water in tomato-soup cans. Customers can take the soup cans if they want, but usually they don't.

"I love dahlias," Rudy sighs. He's staring into a pink flower that's like a cheerleader's pom-pom or a sea anemone. "They're so silly, and..." Rudy leafs through the giant book he carries with him everywhere. He found it a month ago, in the attic, when we first moved to the farmhouse. It's a kind of dictionary called a thesaurus. "...elegant. That's it. They're the only thing that's both silly and elegant."

Hee-HAW.

Rumpley, my donkey, brays from his spot in the field in front of our house. I give Rudy a look. "No," Rudy protests. "Rumpley is not silly, he's awkward. And he's not elegant"—Rudy ruffles the pages of his thesaurus—"he's dignified."

Rudy's my little brother. He's eight. I'm nine. We moved to the country at the start of summer.

When we lived in the city, we'd add water to a can of pink slush from the grocery store, set up a card table on the sidewalk and call it a lemonade stand. In those days, we didn't have dirt under our nails. We never scavenged in barns or pushed each other into bushes or lay in bed at night running our fingers across the thorn scratches on our arms and legs. Our skin was clean, and we only took baths once a week. These days we need baths nearly every night. These days, if we wanted to sell lemonade, I think we'd start with actual lemons.

A dented pickup truck rumbles up in front of our stand. The driver hops out, leaving his keys in the ignition and his door open. His radio is playing a country song that my dad likes:

you and me go fishing in the dark...
down by the river in the full moonlight...

The man is wearing the regular outfit around here—jeans, work boots, white T-shirt under a plaid shirt, and baseball hat, bill in front. "Hi, boys. Your tomatoes look all right. Nice blackberries too. You're clean pickers."

"Cyrus isn't," Rudy blurts.

I shrug. Who cares about a few stems in their berries?

The man squats down until he's eye level with me. "It's important, son. Like getting good grades—"

"I get good grades!"

"Well, not in the picking department." The man stands. He glances at something in the back of his truck. "Boys, I've driven past your stand a few times now. I've been wondering, would you help me out?"

"Sure!" I say.

"Maybe," Rudy says. He's more scared of the world than I am. He also gets hurt less.

"It's like this," the man says. "I've got worms."

Rudy and I shoot each other a look. We had worms a year ago. An awful-tasting tablespoon of medicine cleared them up. It was a few days before I realized we'd drunk worm poison.

"Wigglers," the man says.

"They're itchy," Rudy says.

"Really itchy," I add.

The man gives us a worried look. "I mean *Eisenia fetida*. The Californian earthworm? Red wigglers?"

Rudy and I don't know what to say.

"Look," the man continues. "I bought a pound of the worms a month ago to help break down my compost pile. They eat up all the compost and then they excrete—"

"Excrete?" Rudy riffles through his thesaurus. "Oh."

"—castings," the man continues. "Fertilizer."

"Worm poop," Rudy says. "Manure."

"Indeed. Problem is, my red wigglers are multiplying like crazy. I started with fifty and now I've got thousands. My compost pile is all worms. There's no food left for them to eat. I've been thinking maybe you two could sell them. I don't want the money you make. I just want the worms to find good homes." The man opens his tailgate and slides a large plastic container off the back of his truck. "They're yours. For free."

He lifts the lid. Rudy and I lean in. It's a party in there, a mound of skinny red worms sliding between, under and over each other. It's like live spaghetti.

Rudy gulps.

"Breathe," I tell him. Rudy often gets anxious. Lots of things worry him, but especially surprises. Taking long, deep breaths helps him calm down.

"People won't pay for worms," he warbles. "That's like paying for dirt."

"Maybe we could just give them away?" I suggest.

"No one will take them if they're free," the man says. "First rule of business—nothing says value like a dollar sign." The man hands Rudy a fistful of baggies. "I'll bring more in a few days. Hey, how about I take a bouquet of dahlias in trade? They're so, I don't know, eccentric. Gorgeous too."

Before we can say anything, the man drives away, his truck kicking up a cloud of dust.

Rudy squeezes his eyes shut. I cough and sputter.

Chapter Two

Rudy takes a marker and adds to our sign. **Red Wiglers. $2/Baggie.** As soon as he snaps the cap back on the pen, a yellow convertible screeches to a stop in front of us. A woman in large dark sunglasses dangles a five-dollar bill out the passenger window. "I can't tell you how much I've been needing good worms," she says. "What with the fair around the corner. Two baggies, please."

I lift the lid of the worm bin. Ugh. I look up at the blue sky and thrust a hand into the spaghetti party. I get a writhing handful and thrust it into a baggie. I fill a second one.

"Don't seal the bags completely!" Rudy begs. "Worms have to breathe."

"Keep the change," the woman says.

"Did you mention a fair?" I ask the woman.

"Not just a fair. The Saanich Fair! It's bigger than Christmas." The woman roots around in her purse and hands me a pamphlet. She revs the convertible's engine. "Thanks for the worms, boys!" she shouts as she peels away.

"Well," Rudy says, peering after the convertible. "That was inter—"

Branches snap in the bushes behind us. Birds flap out of the leaves, twittering. "Cougar," I whisper. "Don't move."

"Hey, guys!" Rachel stumbles out, her hair full of leaves. "I hear you're selling worms!"

Rachel is my age. Every day she dresses in one single color from head to toe. From the barrettes in her hair to the shoes on her feet. Pink, green, blue, purple, yellow—any color of the rainbow. Only today, things are different.

"Black isn't a color," I tell her.

"I'm mourning Grandma. People wear black when someone they love has died." Rachel's grandmother died two days ago. She was sick in bed for a long time before that. "Grandpa heard you're selling worms. He wants three bags. He'll pay extra if he has to."

I reach into the slimy party and fill three baggies, leaving the tops partway unzipped. "That'll be eight dollars. Since you don't mind paying extra."

Rachel looks at our sign, does the math and shrugs. She pays the eight dollars, then hurls herself back through the bushes. "See you at Grandma's memorial!"

Rudy makes a choking sound.

"Breathe," I tell him.

Rudy is terrified of the memorial. He's upset about Rachel's grandmother dying, even though we only met her once. We'd been in Rachel's yard, calling for her to come out and play. Cornelia was leaning out an upstairs window, brushing her long gray hair. *"If you want to live as old as me, don't step on spiders,"* she yelled down at us. *"Promise?"* We'd nodded solemnly.

Another car slows in front of the stand. It's sleek and weird—a car in the front, but like a pickup truck in the back. The driver steps out. He's wearing a brown fedora and a three-piece brown suit— pants, jacket and vest—with a mustard-colored shirt and a heavy gold necklace. He tells us the car is a 1969 El Camino.

"Wow," I say.

The man buys three baggies of worms. "Now my tomatoes will be as red and swollen as a man's aching heart. And my onions will make the bravest woman cry." He tips his hat to us. "I'm very thankful to you," he says. I believe him.

Once he's gone, I give our cash box—a yogurt container with a slit in the lid—a shake. "Looks like we're worm moguls."

"Moguls?" Rudy leafs through his thesaurus. "*Magnates. Captains of industry. Entrepreneurs. Tycoons.*"

"Tycoons! This calls for a celebration, don't you think?"

Rudy nods. We gobble down an entire box of blackberries, staining our teeth and lips purple. We drop a few berries into the bucket. The worms devour them frighteningly quickly.

It's getting dark. We pack up the stand for the night, deciding to store the bin of worms in the barn.

"Cyrus?" Rudy croaks as we're turning our sign around. "Look."

I glance up the winding road. A woman is pedaling toward us on a strange contraption. She wears a hooded cloak that ripples around her like dark water. "I couldn't get the car to start," she puffs, leaping down from her seat and trotting past us, holding on to the thing until, with a "Whoa, Nelly" from her, it comes to a stop.

"No brakes," the woman explains. "Penny-farthings don't have them. This was my grandfather's. It's named for the coins. The back wheel is small like a farthing, and the front wheel's big as an old English penny."

"Today, we'd call it a toonie-dime," Rudy says.

The woman's face lights up. She looks at Rudy like she's meeting Einstein. "Exactly!"

Old people usually like Rudy better than me. It's because he doesn't look like he's going to make any sudden moves. Mom says old people's bones break easily.

The woman extends a gloved hand. "I'm Esther." She and Rudy shake. She looks me up and down and furrows her eyebrows. I give her my quietest, politest smile, and finally she puts out her hand. "I hear you're selling red wigglers."

"You are correct. We are selling worms," Rudy says. "Two dollars a bag. And we stuff them full."

Esther lifts the hem of her long black skirt and reaches into the side of a boot fastened shut with a row of buttons. She pulls out a ten-dollar bill. "I'll take four bags. And with the remaining money, how about some of those dahlias? I love dahlias. They're so otherworldly. Yet so lovely. Though yours look kind of pale. You aren't giving them the medicine, are you?"

"Medicine?" Rudy asks.

"The black gold."

"G-gold?"

Esther points to her cape's hood, where she has tucked the four bags of worms. "These worms are alchemists. Feed them rotting leaves, wilted lettuce, apple peels, limp cabbage, carrot tops, pumpkin guts, even used napkins, and they turn it all into gold. Black gold. The best fertilizer known to humans."

Esther starts pushing the penny-farthing up the road, running along beside it. Finally she leaps up onto the seat. As she pedals away, she chants, "Potassium, magnesium, phosphorus, calcium, copper, zinc, cobalt, carbon, manganese, nitrogen..."

"Your dahlias!"

Rudy runs his fastest to catch up and thrusts the flowers into Esther's gloved hand. She tucks the bouquet between her teeth and rides off down the winding road.

Chapter Three

I'm under my blankets, reading with my flashlight. It was lights out ages ago, but I'm studying the pamphlet. What I've learned is that the Saanich Fair is the longest-running agricultural fair in Canada, and it happens every year in our neighborhood on the last weekend of the summer. That's next week! There will be rides, rock bands, dog races and barns full of cows, horses, llamas, chickens, rabbits, pigs, even bees, all competing to be the most beautiful, or the biggest, or the best trained, or the best milk maker or honey squirter. There are tons of contests to enter and lots are for kids— tastiest apple pie, most colorful quilt, most imaginative homemade toy, best painted rock, swoopiest handwriting. You win five dollars if you come in first.

Mom said a few weeks ago that she would help me buy a new bike if I saved $100. I have $60 from the farm stand so far. A cash prize or two would get me closer. I find a pencil and circle the contests I could maybe win. LEGO and Tastiest Cucumber. That's about it.

Chink, chink.

Hail? I throw back my covers and run to the window. Down in the yard is a gray-haired man with a flashlight and an empty bucket. It's a friend of Rachel's grandpa. Delmar. "Are you the boy that's selling worms?" he booms.

I put my finger to my lips, then signal I'll be down in a second.

Mom is doing homework at the kitchen table. She's working on her PhD, which is a big university degree. Lately, Mom has her head in her books all the time. Which was one reason Rudy and I decided not to tell her about the worms. She doesn't need more to worry about. I mumble that I've forgotten to give Rumpley his water and slip out the kitchen door.

Delmar follows me to the barn. He shines his flashlight so we can see where we're going. I scoop four handfuls of worms into his bucket. We're starting to run low. He gives me eight dollars, says thanks and vanishes into the woods.

Without the glow from Delmar's flashlight, the yard is darker than my closet with the door shut. The darkness is thick. It presses against me like it wants to tell me something. It fills my pockets.

I put my hands out in front of me so I don't walk into anything. If an outside light came on, I'd look ridiculous,

shuffling across the gravel like a zombie. An owl hoots. Something rustles in the bushes. My heart thuds. A bear?

Finally the back door is in sight, its window yellow with the light from the kitchen. I hurry up the stairs so fast that I bang my shin badly on the last step.

But I barely feel the pain. I'm too relieved to be inside. Mom doesn't even notice me. She calmly turns a page of her textbook, then reaches for her tea. But I notice *her*. My heart slows right down.

Chapter Four

Rudy and I are sold out. The worm customers are getting impatient. We take down their phone numbers and promise to call when we get more. A worm wait-list. Luckily, the worm man drops off another bin during the night. When Rudy and I get to the stand in the morning, crows are pecking at the lid, trying to get in. How do they know worms are inside? Can they hear them?

Can they read their minds? Do worms *have* minds?

We hole up in a closet where Mom won't hear us and call everyone on the wait-list. Then we drag a basket of LEGO down to the stand and work on our fair entries between business transactions. We're both entering the *LEGO Builders* category. Rudy is making a model of a human heart. He's figured out how to make it smooth and round.

He's also entering *Smocking: Boys, 7-11*. Smocking is a kind of sewing that cinches clothing into tight ruffles. Rachel's grandmother was a smocker. She taught Rachel the basics, and Rachel passed them on to Rudy in exchange for a carton of blackberries.

Remembering her grandma made Rachel sad, and then she pricked her finger with the needle and started to sob. Rudy and I patted her on the back. She was still all in black, including a black knit cap—in the summer—and black toenail polish. I have to hand it to Rudy though. I am guessing that his smocking category won't get many entries, which gives him a good chance of winning.

Rachel is entering two categories, *Laying Hens* and *Brown Eggs: Dozen*. Rachel and her grandpa keep hens and sell the eggs. Mom says they're the most delicious eggs in the world. Dad boils up a dozen to take when he goes to camp. Dad's a west-coast logger, which is the world's most dangerous job, more dangerous than being a trapeze artist. He's often away, operating a feller buncher, a machine that does what it says it does—*fells* trees, then *bunches* them into gigantic bouquets. Dad's strong and enormous. He probably eats all twelve of those eggs in a day.

It was easy to find out on the Internet how to look after the worms. I've been tossing kitchen scraps—peels, cores, brown lettuce leaves, scavenged from the compost bucket in the kitchen—into the worm bin for the worms to eat. Then I harvest the "castings"—a polite word for poop—and add them to my garden bed,

31

focusing on the area where my best cucumber grows. I've named him Cuke. He's my ticket to winning five dollars. Cuke outshines the others. The good stuff from the castings has made him dark green and sturdy.

On Friday morning, Rudy bites the end of the thread he's using to smock his shirt and ties a knot. "Well, that's done." His T-shirt used to say *Camp Thunderbird*, but now that it's smocked, it says *Cmtudrid*.

"Sounds like the name of a Viking warrior," I tell him. He likes that. Today's the day to get our contest entries in. Rudy finished his LEGO heart a few days ago, and I'm nearly done my LEGO Wild West town. Well, not a town really. I only got the saloon done, but the swinging doors work great.

Time is gobbling up the last few days of summer. Tomorrow morning is Rachel's grandma's memorial, and then we head to the Saanich Fair for the day.

Then it's school. Mom took Rudy and me to Burt's in town for haircuts. Burt teased us about the dirt in our ears. *Country boys*, he called us. But he gave us lollipops like he always does from his big glass jar. As usual, I checked mine over for hairs before licking.

Halfway through the morning, the worm man pulls up and drops off half a bin. "That's the last of them," he says. "I want to thank you boys for helping me solve my worm dilemma."

"*Dilemma.*" Rudy flips through the pages of his book. "*Predicament. Quandary. Problem.*" He looks at the man. "Anytime."

Later, as I'm slotting the last brick into my saloon roof, Rudy elbows me. He's breathing funny. He points up the road.

Dad! Back from the bush, running toward us. When he reaches us, he throws his duffel bag to the ground, and Rudy and I leap into his arms. Then, after dangling us by our ankles, he sets us on a high tree branch.

As we beg for him to get us down, he sizes up our roadside stand. "What's in there?" he asks, pointing at the worm bin.

"We haven't told Mom," Rudy stammers.

Dad scratches his head. "Is it dangerous?"

"No."

"Immoral?"

Rudy flips through his thesaurus. "*Corrupt. Dishonest. Wrong.*"

"No," I answer. "It's not immoral."

"Illegal?"

Rudy starts flipping through his book.

"No!" I shout.

"Well then, you don't have to tell me what's in there."

"Really?" Rudy asks.

"Really," Dad said. "As long as no one is getting hurt or doing something wrong or breaking the law, then it should be fine."

"It's worms," I blurt.

Dad laughs. "Long, thin, slimy ones or short, fat, juicy ones?"

"Red, wriggly ones," Rudy says. "The Californian earthworm. *Eisenia fetida.*"

"They sell well," I say. "People like them in their gardens. Their tunnels get air and rainwater deep in the dirt, and they loosen up the soil so plants can grow more easily, and they eat rotting plants and poop out castings that are full of good stuff. Black gold, it's called—"

"I don't know about all that. I'm a logger, and what I know is you don't want worms in the wood. But to each their own." Dad grabs his duffel bag. "I picked up some groceries on the way home. I better get them in the fridge and say hello to Mom."

"Dad?" Rudy asks.

"Don't worry. I won't tell her. She has enough on her plate. She doesn't need worms on there too."

Chapter Five

It's time to cut Cuke loose from the vine. Will he miss his garden, his bed? Like I missed our old home when we first moved here? I open the scissors. "This might sting," I whisper. *Snip*. Nice and quick. Cuke falls to the dirt. Poor thing. I tuck him into my pocket, thinking of those pictures of Mom carrying us as babies in a sling.

I head inside. A cucumber that Dad got at the grocery store is lying on the kitchen table. I pat Cuke. Cuke is a lot smaller than the one Dad got. Before I know it, I've grabbed the huge store-bought cucumber and run up to my bedroom. I close the door. A little sticker on the cucumber says *Mexico*. So it's a Mexican cucumber. I name him El Cucumbro. I pick the sticker off and press it onto Cuke.

"Time to go!" Mom calls from downstairs. We're heading to the fairgrounds to drop off our contest entries.

"Coming!" I answer.

As I pass through the kitchen, I place Cuke on the kitchen table, right where El Cucumbro had lain. Cuke looks pathetic, shriveled and bumpy, but Dad won't notice. Dad's so huge, every cucumber is small to him.

I try not to think about my switcheroo as we drive to the fairgrounds. It's too late anyway. Cuke is getting farther and farther away.

Rudy is crying because he thinks his smocking is uneven.

"Rudy, you've got to look at the big picture," I tell him. "I can't even do one stitch. You must have done a thousand."

"One thousand, three hundred and nineteen," Rudy sniffs.

"That's serious dedication," I say, feeling a pang. I'd been dedicated to Cuke. I *sang* to Cuke. I gave him castings every day, mixed them into the soil around him, watering afterward so all the magnesium and copper and nitrogen

flowed down into his roots. But El Cucumbro? We hardly know each other. "You've stood by your T-shirt, Rudy. That's really something."

"*Stood by my T-shirt*?" Rudy says. "What the heck is that supposed to mean?"

"He means you have been committed to it," Mom clarifies, looking at Rudy in the rearview mirror. "You saw it through."

"Like if Cyrus had finished his Wild West town," Rudy sniffs.

"Hey!"

"Oh, look," Mom says. "We're here."

Chapter Six

Mom pulls off the highway and onto a field that a week ago was probably waist-high with hay. It's harvest time. That's the kind of thing you can smell when you live in the country. The car bumps over hay stubble toward a half-built Ferris wheel, stick arms raised in the air, waiting for seats. That's one thing about living in the country—you get to go off-road. Now when I'm in the city and

I see a house with cars parked right on the lawn I think, Those people have lived in the country.

We pull up beside a battered car with a muddy shovel handle sticking out of a side window. Rudy points to a bumper sticker that says *My Other Car is a Penny-Farthing*. I wink at him.

Inside the fairgrounds, people are coming and going with apple pies and jars of pickles and chickens in cages in their hands. Horses and cows are being coaxed from trailers. A small crowd chases an emu that has gotten loose. Mom won't let me join in. We leave our LEGO projects in the Children's Gallery, and then Mom points me toward the Agricultural Hall to register my cucumber before she and Rudy submit his smocked shirt at the Textiles Barn.

Plates of deep-red tomatoes, potatoes scrubbed to perfection, onions with their tops tied with bows, warty gourds, and zucchinis the size of my leg fill the long tables in the barn. At the back, people work their way up to a desk where a woman takes down their names and categories. The woman is Esther. She's writing swoopy letters in a thick book with yellowed pages. Her capital letters make me think of the lace curtains in Rachel's living room. Rachel says her grandma made them, but I don't believe her. They're just too—where's Rudy with his thesaurus?—fancy.

Finally I'm at the front of the line. "Name?" Esther says, not looking up.

"Cyrus Inglot."

Her hand swoops across the page. The capital C for my first name is like

an inky plume of smoke. The *I* for Inglot looks like an inky fishhook.

"Category?"

"Cucumber," I say.

"Let's see it."

I place El Cucumbro in her hand, thinking how impressed she'll be. I've pretty much forgotten that I didn't grow it.

Sure enough, as soon as it lands in her hand, her face freezes. Her eyes widen. She looks up. "Really?"

"Yup!" I say. "Amazing, right?"

"Amazing, indeed." She looks at me carefully. "I know you, don't I?"

"Worms," I say.

"I thought you said Inglot."

"No, I mean, you bought worms from me and my brother."

Esther nods. Then she searches around in her black-buttoned boot.

She pulls out a knife with a curved blade and a handle like an animal's horn.

"You're going to—?"

"The three judges each need a slice, and as registrar I am to have a slice as well, to confirm that it is indeed a cucumber."

She slices four perfect, thin, pale-green ponds. She picks one up, looks at me and bites. She chews, swallows. "Have you ever heard of *terroir*?" she asks.

"Heard of it? I've *been* terrified. When my family put our house up for sale. And when the tide stranded me on the rocks. And when the olive jar fell on Mom's foot and there was blood everywhere and she fainted and then Dad came in and when he saw her he turned pale and leaned over the kitchen sink and—"

"*Terr-OIR*," Esther interrupts. "The idea that food tastes like where it grew. The idea that you can tell where something grew by how it tastes."

I gulp.

Esther nods. "The dirt and air and water of a place is in the flavor of its fruit and vegetables, even its meat."

"That's silly," I said. "Dirt is dirt. It's the same everywhere."

"No, it's not. Wherever you go, dirt has its own personality—a different mix of minerals and nutrients. Dirt has character."

"You got that right!" someone behind me sings out. "Saanich soil is sweet."

"With a satisfying iron tang," someone else adds.

Esther swoops her pen across her book—ink wind blows, ink waves crash, ink hair coils into braids.

"You have amazing handwriting," I say. "And that book is huge."

"Penmanship," Esther corrects. She raps her knuckles on her book. "Ledger." She waves me aside. "Next!"

I wobble away on mushy knees. My face is hot. But by the time we find Mom, I have convinced myself that Esther was just very impressed by the cucumber I grew. She respects me because of it, and that was why she took the time to tell me about terror. I mean, *terroir.*

Chapter Seven

I wake up on Saturday morning excited about the fair. But then I see my suit hanging from my curtain rod. Dad ironed it yesterday. Right. First we go to Rachel's grandma's memorial. *Then* to the fair.

"What's the point of going to a memorial?" I ask Dad as we chew our granola. "I mean, she's dead. She won't know whether we're there or not."

"No, but Rachel and Jerry will know. Our role is to try and fill the hole that Cornelia left. To show them that there are people who love them and reasons to be happy. We also let them be sad. We're there to say, *Cry, mourn, go to the deepest depths of your sadness. You are safe with us, we see you grieving, and we'll be here when you surface.*"

Mom kisses the top of Dad's head. "Wise old man."

"*Wise man* will do," Dad says, pulling Mom's hand to his lips. The two of them are always lovey-dovey when Dad's first back from camp.

"Let's go," Mom says. "Where's Rudy?"

We look for Rudy in the house and the outbuildings. He isn't in the old pigsty or chicken coop or silo. We're in the barn scratching our heads when *whumpf*—a large book drops at our feet, blowing up dust. We rub our eyes and look up. There's Rudy, perched on a rafter.

"I don't want to go," he whines.

"Breathe, Rudy," we say in unison. Then we all take a deep breath. In through the nose, out through the mouth. And another one. Mom, Dad and me, like some strange breathing choir. Rudy starts giggling.

"Let's get in the car first," Mom calls up.

The best way to deal with Rudy's anxiety is to just think about the small picture, the next step. Rudy is probably up there thinking about death and sadness and crowds, huge things that are impossible to figure out. The goal is to get him thinking about putting one foot in front of the other, about small, real things.

"Let's see which car door creaks the loudest," I suggest. "I think it's the driver's."

"No, it's the right back door," Rudy says.

"Race you there to check!"

Rudy swings down and drops into Dad's arms. Turns out he was right. The right back door is creakiest.

The memorial is held in a church in the middle of a field in the middle of the woods. It's like we're inside the pupil of an eye. Which would be bright, even though it's black. A pupil is dark, but it lets in light. That's its job.

While Mom and Dad coax Rudy out of the car, Rachel says hi.

"You aren't in black!" I say. "You're in a whole bunch of colors! All at once!"

"I figured something out. I was looking out my window last night, thinking that the color black gets a bad rap. The dark is friendly. It's alive, not dead. When I close my eyes at night, I don't go into darkness. I dream. In color. Then I started thinking about Grandma. She was a gardener. She grew flowers and vegetables. She planted seeds, buried them in the dirt, and those seeds grew into dahlias and tomatoes and carrots. Purple, red, orange. All out of the dark!"

"How does it feel to wear different colors at the same time?"

"A little weird. Like I'm crying colorful tears. Grandma was tons of fun. She taught me how to do cool stuff, like knit, sew dolls, churn ice cream, even how to waltz!" Rachel rises up on her toes and does a pirouette.

Rudy does well during the service. He sits up straight and catches his tears tidily with his tongue. After the minister goes on about Cornelia's life, we gather around a small hole in the ground. Rachel places a box in the hole. It holds her grandmother's ashes. Then Rachel and Jerry plant a tree on top of the ashes. Jerry shovels dirt into the hole and wipes his face with his handkerchief. I think maybe he is wiping off sweat, as he often does, working around the farm. But no. He is crying. Seeing him cry makes me cry.

Then it is time to pile into the car and head to the fair. That is a relief. "From sadness to joy," Dad says. "Zero to a hundred."

Chapter Eight

The first order of business is seeing if we've won any ribbons. And we have! My LEGO saloon has an honorable mention. *Nice engineering on the saloon door,* the judges wrote. Rudy's LEGO heart has a blue ribbon—first prize! For his age group. The competition was tougher in mine. Rudy's smocked T-shirt also has a blue ribbon. There is only one other entry in *Smocking: Boys, 7-11*—some kid has smocked a Vancouver Canucks pennant so it now says *VnovrCncs*. *Nice, even stitches*, the judges wrote beside Rudy's entry. *Next time, try a lighter cotton.*

In the Agricultural Hall, swollen El Cucumbro sits on a Styrofoam plate, surrounded by small, dark, bumpy cucumbers that look like Cuke. They've got ribbons and lots of comments. *Great flavour! Perfect crunch. Sweet peel. Congratulations.*

El Cucumbro has no ribbon and only one comment—*Impossible.*

"What do they mean?" Rudy asks. "Your cucumber is obviously the biggest one. It's smooth too. Not all pimply. But it's pale. And has weird yellow patches. The others look tastier."

"A cucumber is a cucumber is a cucumber, Rudy."

"That's where you are wrong," says a voice. Esther has crept up behind us. She looks me in the eye. "What would your life be like if Rudy wasn't in it?"

My heart sinks. "It would be—nothing. Nothing like what it is."

"And if you lived in a different part of the world?"

"I do live in a different part of the world. In the country. I used to live in the city."

"Have you changed since you moved?"

"Yes! A lot." I kick off my shoes and peel off my socks. "See? Dirty feet. They're always dirty now, because I'm usually barefoot. And look!" I push up my sleeve. "I'm crosshatched from thorns and twigs."

"So you look quite different since you moved to the country."

"Yeah, and I don't get my hair cut as often, because Burt's Barbershop is farther away now. My hair is lighter too, from all the sun. And Mom says I have better skin because we eat more fresh food, especially berries."

"So where you are affects what you look like."

"Uh, yeah."

While Esther launches into a sermon about Saanich soil and water, I work my hand toward the judges' comment card beside El Cucumbro. Maybe I can remove the entire Styrofoam plate too—remove El Cucumbro even. Just make it all vanish.

Esther lays her hand on mine. My face prickles. "You can't take it back," she says. "You can apologize and make amends, but what is done is done."

Rudy looks back and forth between us. "What are you—?" he starts.

"It's between me and your brother," Esther says. "And maybe"—her face lights up—"the queen! Here she is!"

Esther grabs a young woman in a western shirt and cowboy boots, with a large ribbon over her shoulder that says *Queen of the Fair*. "Melissa, I have a job for you."

Melissa blinks. "For me?"

Esther whispers into her ear. Melissa purses her lips and nods. "Got it."

"What?" Rudy says.

"They think I should have won, that's all," I say. "I mean, obviously my cucumber is bigger than the others."

A crackly voice over the loudspeaker announces a spelling bee in the Tea Room. Rudy's eyebrows shoot up. "Go!" I tell him. "I'll meet you there. Remember, *i* before *e* except after *c*."

"Except for some weird exceptions," Rudy says, whatever that means.

The Queen of the Fair lays her hand on my shoulder and steers me toward a small room in the back of the hall. "My office," she says. I sit on a plastic milk crate. She settles onto a haystack behind a battered door laid across two sawhorses.

"Nice desk," I say.

"Look, I wasn't trained to deal with this kind of situation. You have breached

the honor system and broken the trust. Not to mention what you've done to your self-respect." She starts fiddling with the doorknob sticking out of the desk. "I need to come up with the appropriate punishment. Natural consequences."

"Natural consequences?"

"The punishment should fit the crime." Queen of the Fair looks out her office's grimy window. Her face lights up. "Well, look at that. The horse stables. We need them cleaned before the end of the day. All you'll need is a shovel and a hose. And a bucket."

"That doesn't fit the—"

"No, but as far as consequences go," the Queen says with a smirk, "they'll be very natural."

The stables are stinky, sloppy and buzzing with flies. But I clean them well and put down a fresh bed of straw for the horses too, which they immediately pee on. "That's what a horse does when she's happy," the Queen explains. She takes the shovel from me. "Good job. Your crime is atoned for and forgotten. You are dismissed."

I feel better. The only thing I want is to see dear Cuke. Is he still alive?

I find Rudy perched high on one of the prize pumpkins, a third blue ribbon pinned to his shirt. *Spelling Champion*, it reads. The word that clinched the deal? *Heifer*. A young female cow.

"*E* before *i*," Rudy says, gloating.

I jump up onto another of the prize pumpkins.

"You stink!" Rudy says.

"Thanks."

We watch the crowd for a while—little kids crying in their strollers, teenagers looking nervously at each other or into their phones, farmers in baseball caps talking about beef. A kid in faded jeans, a jean shirt and a jean jacket climbs up beside us on another prize pumpkin.

I kind of recognize him. "Hey."

"Hey."

"You live on Cove Road, don't you?"

"How'd you know that?"

"I live in the house with the donkey out front. I've seen you walking your dog."

"Rex."

"Cyrus."

"No, Rex is my dog. I'm Griffin."

"Cool."

"What grade are you in?"

"Five. You?"

"Five too. At Salish Elementary."

"Maybe we'll be in the same class. I'll be new there."

Rudy yelps. "Breathe," I hiss at him. He's nervous about starting at a new school. I hear him take a few deep breaths.

Griffin is counting some coins in his fist. "I'm looking for a birthday present for my dad, but I can't find anything."

"What does he like?"

"Fishing. And that's about it."

"Maybe he'd like some bait," Rudy says, winking at me. He wiggles his baby finger.

Right! "We have the best worms this side of the Rockies. Red wigglers. Two dollars a bag," I tell Griffin.

"I've got $5.50."

"Since we're in the same grade, I'll give you fifty cents off. Three bags for $5.50."

"That sounds good. Can you bring them to school on the first day?"

"Will do."

Rudy and I quickly spend the $5.50 on ice creams—they only have "classic" flavors at the fair. Rudy gets maple walnut and I have rum and raisin, which is awful. Then we meet Mom and Dad at the blacksmith's and head to the car.

As soon as we get home, I check the crisper drawer of the fridge. Yes! Cuke is okay. He looks cold though. I wrap him in a tea towel and take him up to my room. I don't know what I'll do with him. For now, I just want to hang out with him and figure out a way to apologize for not recognizing his awesomeness.

Chapter Nine

Our new school is huge! I had to help Rudy put one foot in front of the other all the way from home to the school, but as soon as he walked through the front doors, he was fine.

"It's just a school," he said, looking around at the hubbub of teachers and kids.

"Of course it is!" I laughed. "What did you think?"

"I didn't know. I think that's what makes me nervous. When I don't know."

I wasn't nervous. I make friends fast. I'm fine on my own too. I'm comfortable in my own skin, as Mom says. Which I've never understood. Are some people comfortable in *other people's* skin?

Fifth-graders get their own lockers at Salish Elementary. With a combination lock. Griffin, the kid from the prize pumpkins, isn't in my class though. I've got the three baggies of worms for him in my backpack. At lunch I ask around, and a kid leads me to his sister, who tells me Griffin's at home with pinkeye.

I'm not sure what to do with the worms. I decide they'll be okay in my locker overnight. I stuff my gym shorts into the vent slots on the door so it's totally dark for them. I stick my head inside to check. Yep, dark enough for worms. Rachel, wearing a rainbow of colors, comes along just as I come out. "You could suffocate in there," she says, tsk-tsking. "A kid needs to breathe."

The next day Griffin is still sick. Now he has whooping cough, his sister says. Poor guy! I leave the worms for a second night in my locker. I save a few of my lunch carrots for them, so they have something to keep them busy.

Day three, Griffin still isn't at school. His sister says he has something called fifth disease.

"Could he be back at school tomorrow?"

"Yeah, sure. Anything is possible," she says.

I decide to leave the worms in my locker one more night. If Griffin's not at school the next day, I'll take them home. I save the lettuce from my sandwich for them. I whisper goodbye before I shut my locker door.

But the next morning when I reach my locker, the lock is gone. My heart pounds. Inside, things have been moved around, and the worms are gone. Gone! Who would steal my worms? The custodian? The librarian? She has dirty fingernails. She's a gardener for sure...

"Cyrus!" A tall woman with very straight eyebrows and dark-red lipstick is heading toward me. "I'm the principal," she says, putting out her hand.

"Cyrus!" Mom calls, coming from the other direction. "I just got a disturbing phone call." She's out of breath.

"The office says you have *worms* in your locker. Three bags of them."

I turn to the principal. "How did you—?"

"We smelled them," the principal says. "We cut the lock, found the baggies and did some research. *Eisenia fetida*. Fetida. From *fetid*. Foul-smelling. Stinky."

"They were stressed, it appears," Mom says.

"When red wigglers don't have enough liquid, they produce their own," the principal says. "A yellow juice that smells like urine."

"Worm pee," I say.

"Yes," the principal says. "The custodian, Ms. McBrian, had the good fortune—I'm joking here—to get a whiff as she mopped the floor last night."

"*Worms*, Cyrus?" Mom says. "Can you please explain?"

Where do I start?

The principal invites us into her office, and I tell them everything, back to that first day by the road when we added worms to our roadside market wares. Then I tell them about Griffin's dad's birthday and Griffin being bedridden with a bunch of medieval diseases. Halfway through my explanation, Dad walks in.

"It's only worms, Edie," he tells Mom.

"*Only* worms?" Mom cries. "Wait. You knew about this?"

"We didn't want to distract you from your postgraduate work."

"What other secrets are you keeping from me?"

"None," I say. "Except—" No, I can't tell her about El Cucumbro. I'll tell Rudy.

I'll come clean to him. "Except—I love you." I smile at Mom.

"Nice try," she says. She looks at Dad. "How about you? Any secrets?"

The principal clears her throat. "It does sound as though Cyrus had good reasons to have the *Eisenia fetida* in his locker. A kindness to a classmate."

"A business transaction, actually," I say.

"Look, how about you deliver the worms to your ill classmate at his house? That seems like the reasonable thing. And remove everything from your locker and clean it out with lemon and vinegar and baking soda and a drop of lavender."

"Natural consequences," I say.

Dad tousles my hair. Mom gives me a funny look.

"Worms are cool, Mom. If it wasn't for their poo, the world wouldn't be as colorful as it is."

"Okay, I get it. Thank you for letting me concentrate on my thesis."

The principal disappears for a moment. She returns with a big Tupperware container. "I've fed Eisner and Esmeralda and Eisa and Fidelis and Fyodor and Fortino—well, all of them—some apple cores from the lunchroom compost. And I added some water." She slides the container across her desk. "And here is your lock."

"Thank you," I say.

"Just give me a bag of worms and we'll call it even."

The principal smiles. Her face transforms. Her eyes glisten, and her hair looks suddenly more alive. *Another* gardener!

Chapter Ten

After supper, I wrap a scarf around my mouth—to protect me from Griffin's diseases—and walk up the road to his door. When I knock, his bulldog, Rex, starts barking. I put the worms—Eisner, Esmeralda and the rest—on the stoop and step back. The man who answers the door is nearly as big as Dad. He wears a hat with hooks dangling from it. A large knife hangs off his belt.

"Ha-happy birthday," I say.

"Well, sure. And what's in the container?"

"A special delivery. Ordered by Griffin. It's a—a birthday present for you."

The man peeks into the container. "Golly!" He cradles it in his arms. "These are lovely worms." He is so excited, he kisses the container! "I'm going to fish the best fish you ever saw fished."

"Good," I say. Then I realize that the worms he loves so much will meet their ends, stabbed through with a hook. Then they'll be eaten up by the fish. And then—well, *they* will become castings. "You could just set them free," I suggest. "In your garden."

Griffin's dad laughs. "They won't catch me fish there!"

"Is Griffin getting better?"

"Sure."

"He has a lot of illnesses."

"Well, actually, he's just scared to go to school. He gets anxious at the start of every year."

"My brother does too."

"Really?"

"Yeah. I just help him get his feet moving. That usually works. Hey! How about if we come by tomorrow morning on our way to school? Maybe Griffin will go if he can walk with us."

"A terrific idea. He'll be so excited to be with friends, he'll forget to worry. Tell you what. I'll make you and your brother a pancake breakfast. Maybe by then I will have caught some fish. Nothing like salmon pancakes!"

"Oh."

"See you at breakfast time!"

When I skip past Rachel's house, I look up at the window and remember Cornelia leaning out of it, brushing her hair, calling down to Rudy and me as if we mattered. How can an entire person disappear?

I think of Rachel and how her hair is just like Cornelia's, thick and dark. So in a way, Cornelia is still in the world. The window is closed and the moon is reflected in its glass. It's high in the dark sky. It looks like a cucumber seed up there.

A cucumber seed! That's what I'll do with Cuke! I'll save his seeds and plant them next year. Esther will be proud of me. Cuke's children can win next year's prize money. But even without winning anything this year, I still earned enough money selling worms to buy the bike I wanted. Now I'm saving up for an El Camino.

The night air smells good, and it's like the dark trees know I'm walking by. It's like they're protecting me. I'm not afraid of the dark anymore. It's full

of amazing things. As Rachel said, it's where the colors get made.

I think of all the worms working away in the dirt beneath me.

Then I run all the way home, light on my feet.

Sara Cassidy is a poet and journalist and the author of nine books for young readers, including *Slick* and *Skylark*. Her books have been selected for the Junior Library Guild, and she has been a finalist for the Kirkus Children's Literature Prize, the Chocolate Lily Award and the Bolen Books Children's Book Prize. Sara has taught at Camosun College and Royal Roads University. *Black Gold* is the third in a series about Cyrus and Rudy, following *Not for Sale* and *Blackberry Juice*. For more information, visit www.saracassidywriter.com.

More Cyrus and Rudy!